Fred

Tio Zé

Dona Rosa

Dolly

Nuno

Nina

Sonia

Gaspar

Bica
and
The Dolphins

Several years ago, when he was only a puppy, Bica had become lost. He had no home. He used to wander about, lost, unwanted and lonely, looking for scraps to eat and somewhere warm to go at night. When he found an old upturned boat, he was glad it had a hole at one end, so that he could squeeze in and fall asleep.

T he boat was owned by a fisherman called Tio Zé. When he and his son, Pedro, found Bica using the boat, they didn't mind. They could see that Bica was lost and lonely and in need of help, so they brought a couple of mats to make him more comfortable. Tio Zé now had a new boat and Bica

kept a close eye on it in return for being allowed to stay in the old one.
Tio Zé and Pedro often invited Bica to go out in the new boat. One day,
while they were out in the bay, a strong gust of wind blew Tio Zé's cap right
off his head and into the sea. "Oh no!" exclaimed the fisherman as he
watched his favourite cap floating away. While wondering how to get it
back, he was surprised to see Bica leap overboard. Bica
swam to the cap, grabbed it and then swam
back to the boat.

Bica was helpful in other ways. One day, Tio Zé pushed his new boat into the water, started the engine and was halfway out into the bay when he realised he had left a bag of fishing gear behind. Bica knew just what to do. He dragged the bag across the sand and swam out to the boat, pulling the bag behind him. Tio Zé was delighted.

So, Bica was a good friend of Tio Zé and Pedro and very happy to have a home of his own. It was clean and tidy and he could come and go as he pleased. One day he woke up, walked onto the beach and stretched. It was another beautiful day. All that was needed to make it perfect was something to eat. Water dogs might be clever swimmers because of their webbed feet, but they are not much good at cooking for themselves. So, Bica bounded along the beach towards the village and Dona Rosa's café.

Passing through the village square, he greeted everyone he met with a wag of his tail. He was pleased to see Gaspar the cat as well as his young friend Nina. Dona Rosa was a very important friend because she always kept tasty titbits for Bica. Her café was always busy at this time of the morning, but Bica was in no hurry. He walked around to the kitchen door at the back and waited patiently.

"Hello Bica," said Rosa when she saw
him. "Just wait a minute or two while I
serve some customers."
It was not long before Rosa came out of the kitchen with
a big bowl of food. Bica wagged his tail and tucked in.
He had almost finished when he looked up and saw Sonia the Stork
noisily clattering her beak and flapping her wings on the edge of her
nest on top of the church tower.

Because she spent so much time high up in her nest, Sonia always had a really good view of the village and the bay. This lovely sunny morning she had noticed something unusual going on and flew out to the middle of the bay to investigate. She could see down through the calm, clear water that a young dolphin was in trouble. It had become entangled in a fishing net and was splashing about trying to get free. "I know who will be able to help," thought Sonia, and flew back to the village to find Bica.

Bica followed Sonia as she flew out towards
the bay again. From the beach he spotted his good
friend Dolly the Dolphin swimming back and forth,
clearly worried about something.

Flying around low over the water, Sonia knew just what the problem was. Bica was not sure because it was all happening quite a long way away, but he realised it must be some kind of emergency. He thought he could probably swim that far, but would he be able to help on his own when he got there? He didn't know the answer to that. What he did know was who he could always count on for help: Tio Zé and Pedro!

Sonia had alerted Bica and now Bica was alerting Tio Zé and Pedro to the problem. The fisherman and his son, who happened to be on the beach, dragged their boat into the water. Bica jumped in after them. The engine roared and off they went as fast as the boat could go.

As they drew close, Tio Zé switched off the engine. Bica jumped out and swam to investigate. He put his head underwater and could clearly see a young dolphin tangled in a fishing net, struggling in vain to get free. Bica grabbed hold of one end of the net and pulled it to the side of the boat. Pedro held on tight to the other end of the net. Bica took a deep breath and dived underwater to straighten out the net so that the dolphin could wriggle free.

It worked! The young dolphin burst out of the net and was delighted to leap free. He didn't go far before turning and swimming in circles around the boat as it headed back to the shore. Dolly joined the young dolphin and the two of them kept leaping in and out of the water to show how happy they were. "I've just made another friend," thought Bica as he watched them.

Overhead, Sonia dipped her wings as if to say "well done". As she flew back to her nest on the church tower, Dona Rosa was waiting on the beach with Bica's young friends Nina and Nuno, who clapped and cheered as the boat neared the shore.

The last thing Bica thought that night before curling up and falling asleep, was how good it was to have really good friends and a really cosy home.